A Red Frog Production, a collection of children's tales.
Like us on Facebook at Red Frog Productions.

ISBN: 978-1544958439
ISBN: 1544958439

Nathan's Tree

A Red Frog Production

Not so very long ago
and not too far from here
lived a little boy named Nathan
who had some childhood fears.

Nathan feared the dark,
and thunder scared him so,
and down into his basement
was a place he would not go.

He feared the kind of spiders
that sit atop their web
and imaginary monsters
that lived beneath his bed.

Shadows made him worry
as they danced across the floor.
He feared things in his closet
that might watch him through the door.

But Nathan didn't fear everything;
outdoors he felt so free,
and in a field one summer day
Nathan found a tree.

A tiny tree, oh so small,
brown and tilted to one side,
leaning down into the weeds
as if to try and hide.

Nathan got down on his knees
and cleared the weeds away.
Then he whispered to the little tree
what he had to say.

"Don't be frightened, little tree,
alone in this big field.
I will help you to be brave
because I know how you feel.

I will come and visit you
until your fears are gone,
and I will take good care of you
until you're big and strong.

I'll do my best to brave,
and I know that you will too.
Think of me when you're scared
and I will think of you."

Nathan came to see the tree
as often as he could,
and very soon the little tree
began to look quite good.

The tree began to grow up tall
but Nathan would still say,
"Just be brave, my little friend,"
as he cleared those weeds away.

As the tree grew taller,
Nathan grew some too.
He was growing on the inside,
as children always do.

Thunder didn't seem so bad,
nor did the spider on the web,
and most of the monsters had moved away
that lived beneath his bed.

If Nathan became a little scared
of things he could not see,
he'd stand up tall and do his best
just like the little tree.

Over the years the little tree
grew beautiful and strong.
And Nathan grew into a man;
his childhood now was gone.

Nathan left to live his life,
as adults sometimes do.
He'd gone into the outside world
to see things that are new.

Nathan's long since moved away,
moved to a distant land,
but he comes back to see the tree
as often as he can.

He sits beneath the mighty tree
in the cool shade of his friend.
Nathan still talks to the tree
and says, "Remember when... ?

When you were afraid
and tried to hide down among the weeds.
When spiders, dark, and scary monsters
were things that frightened me.

"And how I found you all alone,
and in some way you found me.
As you helped me to become a man,
I helped you to be a tree."

Nathan learned from the tree
that when you're standing all alone,
don't hide in weeds, just stand tall,
and you can weather any storm.

Nathan leaned gently back
and rested against the tree,
and in his favorite place of all,
Nathan fell asleep.

What was once a frightened little tree,
now towers high above.
A little tree that almost died
but grew from Nathan's love.

Made in the USA
Middletown, DE
16 May 2017